A Blue Snail Called Sami 一隻叫山米的藍色蝸牛

作者：楊巧翎 Jolyn Yang

出版：巧米文化工作坊 (地址：300新竹市東區關新西街182號6樓 / 電話： 0905077308)

2019年8月初版

ISBN：978-986-98126-0-3

代理經銷：白象文化事業有限公司
401 台中市東區和平街228巷44號
電話:(04)2220-8589 傳真:(04)2220-8505

About the Author 作者簡介

Jolyn Yang 楊巧翎

Jolyn is an English teacher to kindergarten children. She loves to indulge herself in the world of books, especially picture books. One of her dreams is to compose the stories that she makes up for her children into storybooks, allowing even more children to enter the world of picture books created by Ms. Jolyn.

喜歡徜徉在書本，尤其是繪本異想世界裡的幼兒英文老師。夢想之一是把編給孩子們的故事都畫成故事書，讓更多小朋友進入Ms. Jolyn的繪本世界。

A Blue Snail Called Sami

一隻叫山米的藍色蝸牛

Far away from where we live, there exists a small village called Rainbow Mushroom Village.

In the village, there lives a blue snail, and his name is Sami.

很ㄏㄣˇ遠ㄩㄢˇ很ㄏㄣˇ遠ㄩㄢˇ的ㄉㄜ˙地ㄉㄧˋ方ㄈㄤ， 有ㄧㄡˇ一ㄧˊ座ㄗㄨㄛˋ叫ㄐㄧㄠˋ彩ㄘㄞˇ虹ㄏㄨㄥˊ蘑ㄇㄛˊ菇ㄍㄨ村ㄘㄨㄣ的ㄉㄜ˙小ㄒㄧㄠˇ村ㄘㄨㄣ落ㄌㄨㄛˋ。

村ㄘㄨㄣ裡ㄌㄧˇ住ㄓㄨˋ了ㄌㄜ˙一ㄧˋ隻ㄓ名ㄇㄧㄥˊ叫ㄐㄧㄠˋ山ㄕㄢ米ㄇㄧˇ的ㄉㄜ˙藍ㄌㄢˊ色ㄙㄜˋ蝸ㄍㄨㄚ牛ㄋㄧㄡˊ。

All the other snails from Rainbow Mushroom Village live in their mushroom houses, except for Sami.

除了山米以外， 彩虹蘑菇村的每隻小蝸牛都住在蘑菇屋裡。

This is because Sami is bigger than the other snails.

In fact, he is
TOO BIG.

這是因為山米比其他蝸牛還要大。

他實在太大了。

asks: "Sami, do you also live in a mushroom house?"

 says: "No, I am too big for the mushroom house. I live in a tree!"

 問ㄨㄣˋ說ㄕㄨㄛ：「山ㄕㄢ米ㄇㄧˇ，你ㄋㄧˇ也ㄧㄝˇ住ㄓㄨˋ在ㄗㄞˋ蘑ㄇㄛˊ菇ㄍㄨ屋ㄨ裡ㄌㄧˇ嗎ㄇㄚ？」

答ㄉㄚˊ說ㄕㄨㄛ：「不ㄅㄨˋ！蘑ㄇㄛˊ菇ㄍㄨ屋ㄨ對ㄉㄨㄟˋ我ㄨㄛˇ來ㄌㄞˊ說ㄕㄨㄛ太ㄊㄞˋ小ㄒㄧㄠˇ了ㄌㄜ。我ㄨㄛˇ住ㄓㄨˋ在ㄗㄞˋ樹ㄕㄨˋ裡ㄌㄧˇ喔ㄛ！」

The snails from Rainbow Mushroom Village don't like to play with Sami because he looks different, and he lives in a different house.

彩虹蘑菇村裡的蝸牛都不喜歡跟山米玩， 因為他長得不一樣， 而且他還住在跟大家不一樣的房子裡。

They even like to make fun of Sami.

他們甚至還喜歡嘲笑山米。

They are very mean to Sami.

他們對山米很壞。

One day, the snails are playing happily in the playground as usual.

有_{ㄧㄡˇ}一_ㄧ天_{ㄊㄧㄢ}， 小_{ㄒㄧㄠˇ}蝸_{ㄍㄨㄚ}牛_{ㄋㄧㄡˊ}一_ㄧ如_{ㄖㄨˊ}往_{ㄨㄤˇ}常_{ㄔㄤˊ}的_{ㄉㄜ}在_{ㄗㄞˋ}遊_{ㄧㄡˊ}樂_{ㄌㄜˋ}場_{ㄔㄤˇ}玩_{ㄨㄢˊ}得_{ㄉㄜ}很_{ㄏㄣˇ}開_{ㄎㄞ}心_{ㄒㄧㄣ}。

All of a sudden, dark clouds start to cover the sky, and it begins to rain.

突_{ㄊㄨ}然_{ㄖㄢˊ}間_{ㄐㄧㄢ}， 烏_ㄨ雲_{ㄩㄣˊ}遮_{ㄓㄜ}住_{ㄓㄨˋ}了_{ㄌㄜ}天_{ㄊㄧㄢ}空_{ㄎㄨㄥ}，
接_{ㄐㄧㄝ}著_{ㄓㄜ}就_{ㄐㄧㄡˋ}下_{ㄒㄧㄚˋ}起_{ㄑㄧˇ}雨_{ㄩˇ}來_{ㄌㄞˊ}了_{ㄌㄜ}。

Soon, it is pouring in Rainbow Mushroom Village.

All the snails are screaming for help, and Sami can hear the snails from his house.

不久後，彩虹蘑菇村下起了大雨。

全部的小蝸牛都大喊著救命，山米也從他家聽到小蝸牛的求救聲。

Oh no! The village is flooded, and the snails are going to drown!

喔ʊ不ㄅㄨˋ！ 村ㄘㄨㄣ莊ㄓㄨㄤ淹ㄧㄢ水ㄕㄨㄟˇ了ㄌㄜ， 小ㄒㄧㄠˇ蝸ㄍㄨㄚ牛ㄋㄧㄡˊ們ㄇㄣ要ㄧㄠˋ溺ㄋㄧˋ水ㄕㄨㄟˇ了ㄌㄜ！

At this point in time, the brave Sami rushes to the village and saves the snails.

He carries the snails on his back to keep them from drowning.

這時候，　勇敢的山米衝到村莊拯救小蝸牛。

他把蝸牛背在背上，　好讓他們不要溺水。

Sami takes the snails back to his house to rest. He treats the snails to hot tea and delicious cupcakes.

These snails love Sami's cupcakes and tea.

山ㄕㄢ米ㄇㄧ把ㄅㄚ小ㄒㄧㄠ蝸ㄍㄨㄚ牛ㄋㄧㄡ帶ㄉㄞ回ㄏㄨㄟ他ㄊㄚ家ㄐㄧㄚ休ㄒㄧㄡ息ㄒㄧ， 並ㄅㄧㄥ請ㄑㄧㄥ他ㄊㄚ們ㄇㄣ喝ㄏㄜ熱ㄖㄜ茶ㄔㄚ、 吃ㄔ好ㄏㄠ吃ㄔ的ㄉㄜ杯ㄅㄟ子ㄗ蛋ㄉㄢ糕ㄍㄠ。

小ㄒㄧㄠ蝸ㄍㄨㄚ牛ㄋㄧㄡ們ㄇㄣ愛ㄞ極ㄐㄧ了ㄌㄜ山ㄕㄢ米ㄇㄧ的ㄉㄜ杯ㄅㄟ子ㄗ蛋ㄉㄢ糕ㄍㄠ跟ㄍㄣ茶ㄔㄚ。

After the rain stopped and the flood subsided, the kind Sami helps the snails rebuild their homes.

等_{ㄉㄥˇ}到_{ㄉㄠˋ}雨_{ㄩˇ}停_{ㄊㄧㄥˊ}了_{ㄌㄜ˙}， 水_{ㄕㄨㄟˇ}也_{ㄧㄝˇ}退_{ㄊㄨㄟˋ}了_{ㄌㄜ˙}之_ㄓ後_{ㄏㄡˋ}， 善_{ㄕㄢˋ}良_{ㄌㄧㄤˊ}的_{ㄉㄜ˙}山_{ㄕㄢ}米_{ㄇㄧˇ}幫_{ㄅㄤ}小_{ㄒㄧㄠˇ}蝸_{ㄍㄨㄚ}牛_{ㄋㄧㄡˊ}重_{ㄓㄨㄥˋ}建_{ㄐㄧㄢˋ}他_{ㄊㄚ}們_{ㄇㄣ˙}的_{ㄉㄜ˙}家_{ㄐㄧㄚ}。

The snails are extremely thankful and happy.

 says to Sami: "Thank you so much for saving us!"

 adds: "We also want to say sorry to you, Sami. We are very sorry for being mean to you before."

 says: "Sami, you are our hero!"

小蝸牛們都非常感激， 也很開心。

 跟山米說： 「 真的非常感謝你救了我們！ 」

 提到： 「 我們也想跟你說對不起， 山米。 很抱歉， 我們之前都對你很壞。 」

 說： 「 山米， 你是我們的英雄！ 」

Sami and the snails become very good friends
with each other.

山弓米ㄇ和ㄏ小ㄒㄠ蝸ㄍㄨㄚ牛ㄋㄡ變ㄅㄢ成ㄔㄥ非ㄈㄟ常ㄔㄤ好ㄏㄠ的ㄉㄜ朋ㄆㄥ友ㄡ。

They play together.

他ㄊㄚ們ㄇㄣ一一起ㄑㄧ玩ㄨㄢ。

And they have balloon parties together.

也ㄧㄝ一一起ㄑㄧ辦ㄅㄢ氣ㄑㄧ球ㄑㄡ派ㄆㄞ對ㄉㄨㄟ。

They dance together.
他們一起跳舞。

And they take care of the garden together.
也一起照顧花園。

Sami and the snails are like a big family.

They help each other out, and they spend each day happily together.

山ㄕㄢ米ㄇㄧ和ㄏㄜ小ㄒㄧㄠ蝸ㄍㄨㄚ牛ㄋㄧㄡ就ㄐㄧㄡ像ㄒㄧㄤ一ㄧ個ㄍㄜ大ㄉㄚ家ㄐㄧㄚ庭ㄊㄧㄥ。

他ㄊㄚ們ㄇㄣ互ㄏㄨ相ㄒㄧㄤ幫ㄅㄤ助ㄓㄨ， 快ㄎㄨㄞ樂ㄌㄜ的ㄉㄜ過ㄍㄨㄛ每ㄇㄟ一ㄧ天ㄊㄧㄢ。

THE END